THE PARTICLES   (of White Naugahyde)

William Leavitt

1979

THE PARTICLES (of White Naugahyde) was first performed January 26, 2012 at The Annex (of the Margo Leavin Gallery) as part of the Pacific Standard Time Performance Festival, with the following cast:

(In order of appearance)

NINA ALEXANDER	Linda J. Carter
TOM ALEXANDER	Bill Doyle
SUSAN ALEXANDER	Melissa Paladino
RICK ALEXANDER	Casey Sullivan
JACKIE MACIAS	Corinne DeVries
ZONTAL GRABOWITZ	John K. Linton
NARRATOR	Neil Elliot
ANGIE, VINCENT and EDGAR VAN HORN	Kristopher Logan

Directed by William Leavitt and Rob Sullivan
Setting by William Leavitt
Lighting by Christopher Richmond
Music and sound by William Leavitt and Joseph Hammer

CHARACTERS

NINA ALEXANDER
wife and interior designer

TOM ALEXANDER
husband and inventor

RICK
their teenage kid

SUSAN
their teenage kid

JACKIE MACIAS
weekend visitor and structural reflex counselor

ZONTAL GRABOWITZ
electronics tycoon

ANGIE VAN HORN
the neighbor

VINCENT VAN HORN
the neighbor

EDGAR VAN HORN
the neighbor

The living room of a home in a tract of houses at the edge of the edge of the desert, where developments look to be the result of wind-borne spores or seeds. From the outside they're mostly the same, but the interiors are deformed by many varieties of personal taste. In the center of this room are a fieldstone wall of synthetic stone and a white naugahyde sofa. At stage left there is the requisite sliding glass door framed here by chartreuse drapes. Through the door is a patio with deck chairs that suggest a swimming pool. Lamps made of spirals of copper tubing are set on either side of the sofa, and in front if it is a parabolic coffee table. Right of the center wall is a wood-paneled hallway leading to the bedrooms. The entrance to the dining room and kitchen is left of the center wall in the space between the wall and the slider. All is as it should be in a family setting except for the sand that has drifted into the corners of the room and underneath the furniture. Through the open patio door the desert mountains can be seen in the distance.

PROLOGUE

(On the horizon a flare of yellow sun begins to glow brightly, as NINA enters from the kitchen wearing a robe. Birds chirp, but over their cheerful wake-up calls there is a slowly grinding electronic noise, causing her to clasp her hands over her giant-sized ears. She spins slowly.)

N

(exasperated) Tom, please come in here. *(The noise intensifies.)* I can definitely hear it.

(NINA exits down the hallway, and returns with a half-awake TOM in tow.)

N

Listen, the Crosby's Barcalounger. *(The sound stops and starts again.)* There it goes.

T

(humoring her) Not again?

N

It's going into the full extension mode. *(Hand over her mouth, gasping.)* They've never done that before.

T

How do you know? *(starting to leave)* I don't hear anything.

N

Wait, it's more like I feel it in my head. A vibration not exactly a sound.

T

It's not a sound? It's five a.m., why would they be using their Barcalounger at five a.m.?

N

Oh, they use it all the time. And, they've probably got that poor Vlasic girl strapped into it.

T

I'm sure that Vlasic girl can take care of herself.

N

How can you be so sure?

T

I saw her out in the common area lifting weights?

N

That explains the clanking sound I've been hearing.

T

I wasn't paying attention to the sonic aspect of her routine. *(pause)* I'm going back to bed now.

N

Please, we have to do something about this noise. Isn't there some procedure besides town hall where we can resolve complaints?

T

Yeah well, I could call control, but every time we mention something on behavior issues we get dinged. We've had two this week already because of Rick's use of the remote. *(beat)* Why don't you go over and talk to the Crosbys about it?

N

I don't want to talk to them after what they said to the Van Horns.

T

No, that really wasn't very nice to point out the size of your ears to them and then laugh their heads off. *(He chuckles to himself.)*

N

No, it certainly wasn't nice. *(pause)* You wouldn't want to rub my feet, would you?

T

I'm too sleepy.

N

Well OK, go to bed then.

(TOM *leaves.* NINA *tries to stretch out on the sofa, but because of its slipperiness she almost slides onto the floor. As she struggles with her balance, the electronic sound grows louder and more raucous. Finally, she just sits up and stares into space.* TOM *reappears with a toothbrush in his mouth.)*

T

Hey! Someone left the door open last night, and now there's sand everywhere.

N

I don't care about the sand. Rick can use the shop vac on it.

T

What do you want me to do?

N
Do something about that chair and fix the vacuum.

T
It's their chair, and part of the program we agreed to is not to interfere with the lives of our co-experimenters.

N
I suppose sir, that you are correct.

T
Are you coming to bed?

(Lights fade.)

ACT 1

(The same. Mid-morning. SUSAN reclines on the sofa, reading a magazine. RICK enters, slapping his fist into a baseball glove.)

S

I hate this sofa. It's greasy. *(She drags her fingers over a cushion, making a squeaking sound.)* Why can't we just have one of those plaid things like everyone else has?

R

Because we're more advanced.

(TOM enters from the patio, and SUSAN jumps up and grabs his arm.)

S

Dad, can we get a horse?

T

It's not in the budget.

S

How about a new sofa?

T

What's wrong with this one?

S
It feels slimy and cold, like some kind of lizard.

T
It's very durable, and besides it's practically new.

S
That's just it, it'll never get old or warm.

T
Say, that reminds me, do either of you have any idea what your mother's problem is with the Crosby's Barcalounger? She claims that she can hear it three houses away, and that it's keeping her awake at night.

R
Maybe that's why she's been so grouchy.

S
She hates it because it's covered with the wrong kind of material. I think it's some kind of woodgrain or maybe something that really revolts her like plaid.

T
Can either of you hear it?

R
Negative.

(SUSAN *shakes her head.*)

T
So, she just doesn't like the idea of it and she's making up the sound business?

R

I don't think so, because I know for a fact that it's covered in black mohair which is something she likes, maybe?

S

Maybe its because they use the chair to liven up their night life, if you know what I mean.

R

In a Barcalounger? How about a game of catch, dad?

T

I've got a lot of stuff to do right now before the review committee gets here tomorrow. Have you two done your radioation exercises yet?

S

Well, uh no. We've been busy too, and besides they're not working.

T

I should take a reading anyway. *(He passes a Geiger counter over them quickly.)* Are you feeling any brighter or more active since we started them? *(They shake their heads.)* Susan, your reading is noticeably higher.

S *(holding her arm up)* New watch, dad. Sorry.

T You have to keep doing them.

(TOM *opens a door in the hallway and pulls out a display easel with a show card on it. On the card is a diagram of the collision of sub-atomic particles. He then gives them a soft helmet which they put on reluctantly.*)

T O.K. now Rick, you're the proton and when the anti-Proton, Susan, collides with you your path is deflected and you become an electron which takes a slightly curved path like this. *(Points to the diagram.)* Susan, you become a photon and a muon taking a spiral path like this. Let's try it. Susan, start here, and remember flashlight on after contact.

(TOM *directs them into their places, putting his hands on their shoulders.* SUSAN *runs at* RICK *and butts him in the stomach.* RICK *doubles over in pain.*)

T Come on, cut the monkey-shines. Let's do it in slow motion, and concentrate on the mental picture.

(*He positions them, and they collide again, except this time* RICK *trips* SUSAN *as she goes by, causing her to fall to the floor.*)

S
Dad, obviously this isn't going to work.

R
It worked on mom.

S
Yeah, but she started out that way.

T
Watch it.

S
Have you thought about what kind of music these collisions make?

(She kneels in front of the record rack, and pulls out a Martin Denny album. Before she can put it on the player, JACKIE enters through the front door, carrying a suitcase. NINA follows soon after.)

J
Well, hi you all. Is it football season again, so soon?

(SUSAN crosses quickly, and hugs JACKIE. RICK stares at her bosom.)

T
Hi, toots, you look great. *(Hugs her.)*

J
I'm so happy.

N
Rick, stop gawking and take Jackie's bag to the guest room.

(RICK *goes off with the bag.* JACKIE *wanders around the room, looks out into the patio.*)

J

What a great view! I just love your new house.

N

Well, it's not really ours yet. Maybe if we complete our training.

S

Yeah, it must look pretty sweet after all those bean stalks up in Fresno.

J

She does. And, oh my, look at that pool. Lucky I brought my suit.

S

I wouldn't want to go in the pool right now, Daddy has these fish in there.

J

Fish? For what?

S

Oh, they're just catfish for earthquake prediction. They jump out of the water if one's going to happen.

J

I see. That's something you have to think about, I suppose?

N

Please, don't worry.

15

J

(Noticing the sand.) What happened to your floor?

N

Oh, I'm sorry about all the sand. We had this terrible windstorm last night and we can't lock our doors.

(There's a general commotion off stage, the sound of someone cooking, banging of pots and pans, hissing burbling noises.)

N

(She runs around the wall left, stopping in the breakfast nook.) Tom! It's too hot to cook. Let's order out, OK?

R

(offstage) It's me, Mom. I was looking for the peanut butter. *(He enters wearing jeans, and a skimpy tee-shirt. Exit.)*

N

(going into the kitchen) It's in with the survival pack. *(pause)* Jackie, do you want a Coke or something? A Ramos Fizz? I got this new ice blender, it makes really good slush drinks.

J

Mmmmmmmm. Let's go slush drinks.

(RICK returns with a sandwich, and then struts by the patio door.)

J

Why Rick, you're looking so grown up these days.

R

Yeah, you too, *(Trying not to stare at her low-cut top.)* I mean, you look really nice as always.

J
Well, it's nice someone appreciates me.

R
Check this out, Jackie. *(He pulls a device out of his back pocket.)* It's an extended range remote control. I can change the channel from any room is the house. *(He clicks it a couple of times.)*

S
(O.S.) Rick! Cut it out.

R
See? *(pause)* Hey, I thought you were at Valerie's?

J
I want one. Where did you get it?

R
Built it from a set of plans with off the shelf parts, you know. This one's really powerful. I can control all the satellite dishes in the neighborhood, but don't tell, okay? *(He turns a dial, and the lights dim and crackle.)*

(NINA *returns from the kitchen with drinks and a bowl of celery sticks. Intermittent sound of helicopters.)*

N
Rick, turn that down. You know it hurts my ears.

R
It works on a frequency side-band principle similar to …

N
Did you mow the lawn like your father asked you to?

R

Will there be lawns in outer space? *(NINA glares at him.)* Right away, mom sir. *(He salutes her, and then stomps off down the hallway.)*

J

Now, Rick is almost eighteen, isn't he?

N

Sixteen. He's still a baby.

J

(aside) He doesn't look like a baby to me.

N

Gee, it's great to see you here. You must not get a chance to go out much with all your discussion groups?

J

Oh yes, I'm very busy, and its quote, unquote very satisfying, but now I find what I really want ... *(RICK, shirtless, crosses the patio pushing a lawn mower.)* ... action. Rick must have many girlfriends.

N

No, not really. He always seems to be working on some project of his or Tom's.

J

Well, he seems very mature to me. *(long pause)* Do you feel that your breasts are a source of power, Nina? I mean as a mother and all.

N

I don't know. I never really thought about it. We've been so busy lately trying to live right here in our little bubble.

J

But, what is there to do?

N

Just prove that Tom has some scientific ability and live peaceable with others in the compound. We could be in the first group that goes up in the space colony.

J

Don't you miss driving your car?

N

We have a space flight simulator, which is pretty trippy.

J

Don't they check up on you all the time?

N

Well, if we were really in outer space they couldn't do much, could they? We have to report into control once a day.

J

What are those boxes you've all got strapped to your ankles?

N

Oh, they're just our beepers. They go off if we leave the compound.

J

And, shopping, how do you do that?

N

Catalogs, and we grow most of our food hydroponically. The kids take classes through television and computer hookups, so everything's fine, sort of.

J

Oh, it's all so wonderful. *(She breaks up and starts sobbing.)* It makes me feel like I have nothing.

T

(Storming in through the patio door.) Has Rick been using the remote? I just blew another set of circuits, and I was getting so close, and with time running out.

N

(ignoring TOM*)* There, there, it will be fine.

(TOM *heads for the kitchen and stops.)*

T

Anybody want to ... swim? Everything okay, Jackie?

J

(Sitting up and drying her eyes.) Just reminiscing about old times. *(beat)* A swim would be nice, but I hear you have some carp in there?

T

Catfish. They won't bite.

N

Tom, can't you just take them out while Jackie is here?

T

We'll see, but I was just going to say that if you want to take a dip it would be a good time because I have to fire up the transducer, and I don't want to take the chance of cooking anybody. *(Exit.)*

N

We've had a lot of fish dinners lately.

J

I think I'll take a shower.

N

(sweetly) Oh, I'm sorry about the pool. You don't mind, do you? I know you've been on the road and all.

J

It's fine, really.

N

And after that, I want to hear everything. That darn phone again. *(She gets up to answer it, and it rings just before she picks up the handset.)* Hello. No, she's not here. Over at Valerie's. *(Hangs up.)*

T

(Entering from the hallway.) Have you seen that big gray folder with the happy faces on it?

N

Not recently. I think you left it in the Mercury when it went to the shop.

T

Drat. I was sure you had it when we came back from the lawyers. *(Exit.)*

N

Don't think so. Tom, the papayas are under the sink if you want to make a smoothie. We're out of Tiger's Milk though.

T

(offstage) Where's the Tiger's Milk?

N

We're out. *(Sound of a powerful food blender from the kitchen.)* And, you think you got problems?

J

What are these lawyers? You're not talking divorce are you?

N

Oh that pooh, it's nothing. It's our neighbors, the Crosby's. They have this electric chair thing. I can hear every gear, every motor, and I can't sleep.

J

You mean you can hear the neighbor's chair three houses away? That's horrible.

N

I have heightened psychic powers. I can predict when the toast is going to pop, or when the light is going green. I sort of pre-hear things mechanical.

J

I noticed that you were pretty fast getting to the phone.

N

I think it's because of Tom's experiments. They're designed to produce effects, that he can't control. (NINA *notices the vacant look in* JACKIE'S *eyes.*) Come on. You must be bushed. I'll show you your room and get some towels.

J

Yeah, it just hit me.

(*There is a gentle whirring and clanking noise offstage.* NINA *stops, and cups her hand to her ear.*)

N

Wait a minute, Jackie. I think ... Yes. Tom! You'd better come here.

(TOM *appears at the opening to the kitchen drinking a smoothie.*)

T

Now what?

N

Zontal is on his way over. I can hear his car.

T

Well, if he does stop by, tell him I'm not home. I don't

want him snooping around just when I'm close to a big breakthrough on the catalyzer. I sure as hell don't want to share the patent with him.

N

Oh, don't be so anti-social. He can be really sweet sometimes, and besides he might be able to help you figure it out.

T

I resent that.

(NINA *and* JACKIE *disappear down the hallway.* TOM *hurriedly begins picking up the loose papers and books that are lying around. There is the throaty sound of a power car, and the screeching of it to a stop. Car door slams.* TOM *stuffs papers under a sofa cushion. Door chime rings melodiously, and* TOM *slinks over to answer it.*)

T

(gruffly) Who is it?

Z

Tom, it's me Zontal.

(TOM *opens the door slightly and* ZONTAL *quickly squeezes through. He wears the sleazy shirt unbuttoned to the waist and gold chains around the neck look.*)

Z

Thanks. Bleeping hot out there. In here too.

T

(gruffly) Where's your guest pass?

(ZONTAL *reaches into his shirt pocket, retrieves his pass, then throws it over his shoulder on to the coffee table.*)

Z

Your TV work? The game's on. *(He looks around the room quickly.)* The score's tied five all, bottom of the seventh. I was on my way over to Valley Springs to pickup some coaxial, I thought I could make it back in time to catch the end of the game, but couldn't, and I just thought you might be watching the game?

T

Kids are using it.

Z

You got a portable out in the lab or something?

T

Nope, just the radio.

Z

How's Nina?

T

Fine.

Z

Well, I guess I better be going then. Good seeing you, man. *(beat)* Say, you think any of your neighbors might be watching the game?

T
Don't know.

Z
Just thought I'd check. Okay well, say 'hi' to Nina for me.

T
(edging him toward the door) I will.

Z
She's not around I guess, huh?

T
She's been very busy. (ZONTAL *doesn't seem to be going anywhere.*) You know, there's a bar in the first shopping mall on left as you go out that might carry the game if want to catch the end of it. Sorry to be so busy right now.

N
(offstage) Tom! What did you do with that little TV set? Is it still out in the lab? *(enters from the kitchen)* Jackie wants to relax in her room with "The Dukes of Hazzard." *(mildly surprised)* Oh! Hi Zon. I thought I heard voices out here. Tom does talk to himself occasionally, but …

T
It's not working right now.

Z Hi, Nina.

N
That's strange, because you were watching it this morning?

T We had that circuit overload, remember? Fried the transistors. Sorry.

N Can't you fix anything?

T Listen, we'd better let Zontal go, and discuss this later. He's trying to see the end of the game, and has to get to a TV right away.

N What about the Van Horns? They watch everything. *(beat)* And, they've been looking for someone to fix the tracking on there satellite dish after someone, probably Rick, scrambled it.

Z Yeah sure, I'll give it a shot.

N *(steering him toward the patio door)* They'd love it. Second house on the right, the one with the black vinyl drapes, teenage daughter. You can't miss it.

(JACKIE *appears in the hallway, wearing a very short terry-cloth robe.*)

J Nina, I can't ... whoops *(realizing that she is underdressed, she ducks out of sight)* ... I can't find the shampoo.

Z Gee, I'm thinking the game is probably over by now. Maybe I could help fixing the TV set here?

T
Aw, you should probably go help the Van Horns. *(beat)* I can fix a TV.

Z
Yeah well, all right. *(Exit.)*

T
I think we take an immediate evening leave and go into town while Zontal is at the Van Horns.

N
We don't get a town pass for ten days.

T
Let's take one anyway.

N
We can't, and besides Zontal is harmless.

T
But, what you've told me makes me think he's hot for your bod.

N
That's absurd. We roomed together for a whole year and he never made a single pass at me.

T
Child prodigies are often slow to get the facts of life.

N
You're just jealous because he graduated in two years, and it took you five because you were developing your social skills.

T

Did you find the shampoo for Jackie?

N

No, I was still looking when ...

T

I know where it is. *(Starts to leave.)*

N

Tom! She's in the shower.

T

So? Geeeez, you didn't think id was going to walk in on her, did you?

(ZONTAL *enters from the patio.*)

Z

Game's over. Cards three, bums two. Got get the oscilloscope out of the car to check the dish. They invited me stay for dinner, but I don't know? They seem a little odd.

N

Nah, you don't want to eat there. Fix their dish, come back, and we'll go out for dinner. You can meet our friend Jackie.

Z

The one in the hallway? Yeah, okay, sure, why not?

(Blackout.)

ACT II

(Later that evening. SUSAN enter with a large piece of fabric, which she spreads over the sofa, carefully tucking it in to the cushions. She dims the lights, then begins building a spaceship-like structure out of Lincoln Logs on the coffee table. RICK enters with a small black box, which emits a low tone. He surveys the room looking for a place to hide it.)

S
What are you doing?

R
I need a good hiding place for this. Got any ideas?

S
You can't hide things here. You know that. What is it?

R
Ion generator. Built it from a kit.

S
It makes me feel awful, like I could bite heads off mice.

R
(changing the setting) How's that?

S Oooh, weird and ginchy.

R Oh yeah! How weird?

S Like I just kissed someone.

R That's not what I want. *(beat)* Wait a minute, how would you know? I'll bet you never have.

S I have too. *(beat)* I must have.

R *(turning the dial)* Here, let's try this one. I want it to make everyone feel kind of mellow, you know, because mom and dad have been fighting a lot lately.

S I like the other feeling better.

R Which one?

S You know.

R You're too young.

S I am not. Hey! I hear Zontal's car.

(SUSAN *picks up her sofa cover and Lincoln Logs.* RICK *ditches the black box in a potted plant. Exeunt* RICK *and* SUSAN. *A brief moment later* NINA, ZONTAL, *and* JACKIE *enter through the front door. They're linked together doing the bunny hop.* TOM *straggles behind, not attached.*)

J

Come on, gramps.

T

Hey!

(TOM *grabs* JACKIE *around the waist and pulls her away from the others.* NINA *steps away from* ZONTAL, *brings up the lights, and then flops down on the sofa.*)

T

(holding on to JACKIE*)* Well, I enjoyed the evening immensely. Zontal, good seeing you. Let's talk some time. *(Drags* JACKIE *toward the hallway.)*

N

Tom, relax and let Jackie go. We're having fun.

(JACKIE *sits next to* NINA *on the sofa.*)

T

Well, I thought you might like some quality time with Jackie, and since Zontal has to get over to the Van Horns at some point …

N

(Getting up off the sofa.) Oh, Zontal can stay, can't you, Zonnie boy? *(She chucks him under the chin affectionately.)*

T

Zonnie boy? No more for you tonight.

N

Neeah, come on. When do we get some fun? You got your little laboratory and stuff. *(beat)* I'll make my own. *(She heads for the kitchen.)*

T

Nina wait, for the sake of the kids ... *(Follows her into the kitchen.)*

(JACKIE takes a magazine from the coffee table, ignoring ZONTAL who hovers a bit, and then makes a quick move to the sofa. He sits, but catches his foot on the table leg, and ends up in an awkward posture.)

J

(a little irritated) Are you comfortable?

Z

Oh yeah, sure. *(He shifts around into a more natural position.)* Kind of a tight squeeze, the distance between the table and the couch, I mean.

J

I'm sure. (Continues to thumb through the magazine. ZONTAL stares off into space.)

Z

Say, uh, have you seen the backyard here?

J

Well no, I mean only the part I can see.

Z

(professorially) Ahhh, you really should see it. The desert's beautiful at night. (starts to get up) Want to take a look?

J

That's okay. I have all weekend. (She moves to another part of the sofa, away from ZONTAL.) Hey, there's something under this cushion. No wonder it's so un-comfortable. (She reaches under the cushion and pulls out the folders TOM has hidden there.) Aha! Porno, I'll bet. (She thumbs through it.) Oh, too bad. It's 'The action of human vibrations on the hydrolysis of organic salts' by Tom Alexander. Wow, he must be really smart.

Z

I seriously doubt it.

J

Or crazy. Listen to this – 'out of body travel can occur through the psychic recognitions of chemical formulae. It happens when the vibrations of the psychic body differ from those of the physical body.'

Z

Hogwash. And I know for a fact that he got a 'C' in college physics.

J

Gee, you must have been friends for a long time.

Z

Not really.

J

Well, how would you know that then?

Z

Nina told me. You see she and I were roommates in college before she met Tom. We've been good friends ever since.

(TOM *and* NINA *return with drinks in hand, which they distribute.*)

T

(alarmed) Hey Jackie, what are you looking at there?

J

Looks like your science papers.

T

You didn't let him see them, did you?

J

No, but it looks like something that could be useful in my structural reflex counseling. Says here that if a group organizes itself to imitate a chemical reaction, it could undergo ionization and …

(TOM *reaches for the folder.* JACKIE *pulls it back and holds it to her chest.*)

J

Wait, I'm curious about it. You see I've been trying to get my clients to align their ...

T

(Holding his hand out for it.) Maybe later we can talk about it. *(beat)* Zontal, didn't you say you had to go home and feed your salamanders?

J

Salamanders! Yuck. You keep salamanders?

Z

They make really great pets, like they don't bark, bite or need to be taken for walks.

J

(Aside to NINA.*)* Oh Nina, I don't think so.

N

(whispering) One point seven nine eight two five four nine mil.

J

How do you know that?

36

N

He has a radio controlled digital read out on his beeper. I just looked at it.

J

I really hate reptiles.

N

He's very tidy otherwise.

J

I guess you would know.

N

It's not what you think.

J

It never is. *(pause)* Oh what the hell. Tom, hey, let's try your little experiment. How many people to you need to do it, anyway?

T

Tried it and it doesn't work, sorry.

Z

He's right. There's no way anything like what you just described could occur. There exist only atoms and empty space, and our minds have no control over them, whatsoever. Atoms on the other hand can effect our minds. Alcohol is a good example.

J

Oh come on, Zontal sir, don't be such a spoil sport.

Z
You may call me Zon, if you like.

J
All right, Zon, I understand what you're saying, but I would like to see for myself what would happen. *(beat)* We'll need a couple of electrodes. These lamps will do fine. *(She pulls the lamps away from the sofa and places them at opposite ends of the living room.)* And now, a little atmosphere. *(She turns the lights low.)*

N
That's dark enough, Jackie.

J
Tom, you choose a record. We form ourselves into a U-shape first. Nina right here. Zontal next. Tom. Now we start exchanging ions. I took chemistry. I know what this is about. Oxygen goes this way and copper the other. Like a round sort of.

(They do this. SUSAN appears in the hallway for a moment, then leaves and returns with RICK.)

J
Faster everybody, faster.

(Their words become an incoherent wave of sound.)

R
This isn't what I had in mind.

S
Do something. *(tugs his arm)* Change the setting.

(RICK *sneaks over to the black box and twirls the dial. Their chant slows and stops. They relax and then stare into space as if drugged.*)

Z

Hey, like oxygen man.

J

(*excited*) I felt something.

N

Woohoo! That calls for another drink.

(SUSAN *and* RICK *have retreated out of sight.* TOM *stands perfectly still, looking depressed.* JACKIE *slides over to him and puts her arm around him.*)

J

Are you bummed out?

T

Not yet. I know there are a few problems to work out still. (*beat*) Did anyone feel anything beside some cheap physical sensation? Any feeling of neuron alignment or displacement?

J

(*dreamy*) Well, there was something I liked.

T

Can you describe it a little more specifically?

J

A kind of spiral thing, maybe.

T

(*encouraged*) I'd like to try it again, if don't you mind. We have to be more precise about how we pass the ions.

Z

Say Tom, I'm sorry, but I really should go. *(pause)* And say, by the way Jackie, have you seen my car?

J

Did you lose it?

Z

No, I just thought you might want to – it's a Shark eight thousand.

J

Whoa, that's very impressive. It's really not my style though. I'm more of a bug two person.

Z

Anyone ever call you Jay? Good friends call me Zon.

J

Nope, sorry.

Z

Got kind of a nice ring to it, don't you think?

N

(stepping between them) Well Zon, it was awfully nice seeing you. Thanks for dinner and ... see you soon, okay? *(She hugs him.)*

Z

Yeah sure, let's do it again sometime.

T

(giving a mock salute) Night, Zontal.

J

Goodbye Zonnie boy. It was nice meeting you.

(NINA *tries to step away from* ZONTAL, *but can't. They are somehow bonded together chest to chest.* ZONTAL *drops his arms to his side and tries to pull free, but can't.)*

N

It was great seeing you, but we really should say goodnight. *(She puts her hands on his shoulders.)*

(TOM *and* JACKIE *had started to drift away, but stop when they realize* NINA *and* ZONTAL *are still in the same configuration.)*

N

Tom! Something's gone horribly wrong. We're stuck.

T

You've created a polarized field.

(TOM *puts his hands on their shoulders and tries to pull them apart, but can't. He steps away from them and looks toward* JACKIE.)

N

You knew this was going to happen, didn't you?

T

    Of course not. Why would I want to stick you to Zontal?

N

Because you thought then maybe you might get stuck to Jackie.

T

    I swear that this isn't anything like what I predicted would happen. *(beat)* Let me see that book, Jackie.

J

    Stay away from me, Tom.

(JACKIE *holds it out at arms length and gives it to him.*)

T

    (flipping the pages) Beats the hell out of me. *(Stops on a page and studies it.)* I think you formed a molecule.

Z

    I want to use the phone.

N
Okay, mister smarty, what are you going to do before I call a divorce lawyer?

T
Calm down. It's very simple. All we have to do is relax and reverse the current. I'll start copper from this side and Jackie you start oxygen from that end.

(They go through the process again several times. NINA and ZONTAL try to separate themselves.)

N
Nothing, no go.

J
Shouldn't we call the fire department?

T
Very funny. *(pause)* We could be in serious trouble if control sees this. *(He moves closer to them and spreads his arms out as if he is hiding them.)*

N
(she turns toward TOM, *but remains attached to* ZONTAL*)* It's like a girdle of force that moves around us. *(she turns again so that she and* ZONTAL *are back to back)* See, we can move around, but we're still attached.

Z
What's your liability insurance picture like these days, Tom?

N
Don't worry Zontal, he'll think of something. Tom, don't you have some device out in the lab that might help?

43

T

It's such a mess right now, and with the lights out, it could be dangerous.

N

Just try something, please.

T

All right. Jackie, you'd better stay here and keep an eye on them. *(Exit through the patio.)*

N

You idiot! He's going to need a flashlight, Jackie. It's in the kitchen under the sink. Take it to him.

(JACKIE *leaves and returns with the flash light.*)

J

Got it. *(Exit.)*

Z

(winking at NINA*)* I wasn't sure what Tom had in mind when he said he wanted to experiment. Hee, hee.

N

Don't get any ideas, Zontal.

Z

How long to you think they'll be gone?

N

When Tom goes out to the lab you can never tell what's going to happen.

Z

I see. And, what do you think they're doing out there?

N

(sternly) You know Zontal, maybe it's time we had a little talk, just the two of us.

Z

This is the chance I've been waiting for.

N

Are you familiar with phase tone interior decorating?

Z

No, can't say that I am.

N

It's a project that I've been working on for many years now, and I could really use your input, and perhaps your marketing expertise.

Z

Gee, I'd like to help, but …

N

It's used to balance one's psychological state with the physical environment. For instance, what one has to do is make a mental picture of plants and flowers in natural settings, and with the imagined forces of nature operating on them.

Z

… maybe this isn't the place to talk about it.

N It's okay, we can go in the kitchen if you want. *(they shuffle slowly toward the hallway)* Here, try this; 'Visualize a fresh, seaweed scented shore. The tide is far in the distance, and the sound of waves lap softly on the white sand ...' *(They disappear down the hallway. Blackout.)*

ACT III

(ANGIE, VINCENT and EDGAR VAN HORN enter stealthily from the patio. They wear mechanics coveralls and Ed Hardy hats, otherwise they look exactly like NINA, TOM, and RICK, except that VINCE has ears like NINA'S, and ANGIE'S ears are normal sized. ANGIE carries a plate with a hamburger on it.)

Hey Mr. big shot scientist, your hamburger is ready. Ack! Take a look at that sofa, will you. And these people claim to be so hot with furniture like that? Who do they think they are, anyway?

(VINCE swivels his head slowly as if scanning for signals.)

V

They're definitely the ones who've been screwing up our TV reception. They got devices stashed all over the place. (He homes in on Rick's box in the planter.)

A

I'd like to rip that sofa to shreds. So damn snooty.

E

Yeah, let's mess them up. Huh, how 'bout it mom, dad?

A

Or, even better, we could get them kicked off the project.

V

How we going to do that? They're such damn nice people, like their beds are always made.

A

Boy, you know everything about them, don't you.

(EDGAR *peers down the hallway.*)

E

Yeah, I'd like to know more about that Susan.

V

Yeah, we're supposed to know about each other in the group. It's part of the program.

A

Oh yeah, you mean to hell with privacy? And, what about that hanki-panki out in the lab with the electric lounger?

V
That's the Crosby's.

A
You know that too?

V
I can hear her yelling about it.

E
I think I saw them once.

A So?

V
Well, let's just suppose something were to happen to it. Who do you think would get the blame, huh?

A
Maybe, but now I want to know what you're doing hanging around here listening to her complain about activity in the Crosby's lounger?

V
I wasn't hanging around here. All you have to do is listen and you can hear her whining for miles.

A
Yeah, like I suppose it's the same way you always know when Mrs. Miller has a new bathing suit? *(beat)* Your story stinks, Vince.

E
Take it easy, mom. He's only trying to help.

(JACKIE *appears at the patio door unseen by the Van Horns. She gasps in fright and disappears.*)

A
You always take his side, Edgar. (EDGAR *goes into the hallway*) And, don't be snooping around like your dad.

E
I wasn't snooping, ma.

(*They drift out through the patio door.* JACKIE *follows them at a distance.* NINA *and* ZONTAL *return from the kitchen and stand back to back down center.* ZONTAL *stirs a hot chocolate and* NINA *sips a cup of tea.*)

Z
I never realized Tom was so jealous of me.

N
Ever since I told him about our communal dorm experiment.

Z
We were pioneers though. They would never try anything like that today.

N
Oh, why not?

Z
Because nobody got any work done. All we did was sit around and talk and watch TV. They wouldn't allow that now.

N
But you worked all the time?

Z
I couldn't with so much going on – that's why I flunked.

N
You did? I thought you transferred?

Z
I did – to a job in a warehouse.

N
And I thought that you knew everything.

Z
So did I, but by the time I realized it, it was too late to catch up, and I went into business.

N
That's terrible.

(RICK *enters with his remote control device.*)

R
Anybody seen the TV guide or the remote? Hey, what's the problem here?

N
No problem.

R
Why are you standing like that? Where's dad?

(SUSAN *enters.*)

N
Your father stuck me to Mr. Grabowitz, it seems.

S
Yuckorama. What procedure were you following?

N
Hydrolysis reflux. He says it flipped states, and the rebate caused us to form a molecule?

S
Hydrolysis is relatively safe, at least that's what he told us.

(RICK *scans the room with the remote, coming to rest on the hamburger on the coffee table.*)

R
Hey, where'd that come from? I thought you went out to eat? Did you bring it back for me?

Z
Oh, that must be mine, my reward for fixing your neighbor's satellite dish.

(ZONTAL *reaches for the hamburger, but since he's attached to* NINA, *he can't.* RICK *turns the remote on them and* ZONTAL *comes loose and almost falls head first into the plate. He manages to right himself in time with a spinning move that seats him on the sofa in front of it. He grabs the burger and bites in to it ferociously.* TOM *enters from the patio.)*

T

I couldn't find anything out there on our problem. Hey, you're apart. What happened, honey?

N

(proudly) Rick used his homemade remote on us.

T

Let's see that. (RICK *hands it to him.)* You made it?

R

Yeah, see it works on a frequency side-band principle similar to the ones our brains use to communicate.

T

Frequency side-bands?

R

The alpha pattern, you know.

T

Sure, of course, vector matrixes and ...

N

And, what were you doing out in the lab all that time? You're acting awfully cheery and smug.

T

I got sidetracked programming the sprinkler system waiting for Jackie to bring the ...

N

Oh! Where is she?

S

I think she's at the Van Horns. They were here earlier.

(The sound of the Barcalounger starts. NINA screeches and covers her ears.)

N

Oh no, please, not again.

(The sound continues for a while, then stops with a series of breaking and splintering clicks. Silence.)

N

You kids go to bed. Now.

SR

Aw gee, mom, we're not sleepy and we want to know.

N

Go!

(They leave grumbling about her on the way out.)

N

And Tom, you didn't see her?

T

Not really. I thought she was with you. *(beat)* And if the Van Horns were here, where were you and Zontal, huh, anyway?

Z

(slightly irritated) In the kitchen, Tom. Nina was kind enough to make me hot chocolate.

N

We should go look for her. Let's go, Tom.

T

But, Zontal's in …

(NINA *pulls* TOM *out through the patio door.* ZONTAL *makes himself comfortable on the sofa while looking through the folder* TOM *left there earlier. He kicks off his shoes and stretches out.* JACKIE *enters moments later carrying a large swatch of black mohair.*)

J

Oh, you still here?

Z

Apparently so. *(beat)* Hey, where'd you get that?

J

You didn't see the zombies who just walked in here? Of course not, you were in the kitchen with Nina doing something. Well, I followed them back to their place to see what they were up to, but I lost them. They just vanished, and on the way back I found this over by the pool, on a chair. *(She spreads the cloth over the sofa, then sits at the opposite end from* ZONTAL.*)*

*(*SUSAN *and* RICK *appear in the hallway.)*

S
Darn, they're still here.

R
Man, it's like living in a bus station around here.

*(*RICK *leaves and comes back with a small portable TV which places on the coffee table in front of* JACKIE *and* ZONTAL.*)*

R
Hey, sorry to bother you, but there's this really great show that you might want to watch.

(Exit RICK *quickly.* JACKIE *and* ZONTAL *hardly have time to react, but gaze at the TV.)*

Z
(Fingering the fabric.) Classic black mohair, don't see that much any more.

J
Now, how do you know something like that Mr. Scientist?

V.O. from the TV
"Picture the forms of great rocks jutting out into the sapphire-like sea, their bases washed by creamy foam and snowy spray. Far below lies a dark tunnel with deep Green water dashing through the opening. Over the piled rocks cluster Orange lichens and above the high watermark Purple thrift grows in every cranny."

(Their attention drifts toward the TV set.)

Z

(his speech slows) Nina, it was Nina, she studied interior ...

(They yawn and fall asleep sitting up. RICK returns for the TV and on his way out, he dims the lights. TOM and NINA enter from the patio quietly and warily, as if they were expecting someone.)

T

Can you believe it, someone completely dismembered the Crosby's Barcalounger? That noise you heard, remember? We could get blamed for it.

N

I wouldn't worry, and besides it's quiet now, isn't it? Come on honey. *(She leads him toward the hallway.)*

(They realize JACKIE and ZONTAL are on the sofa.)

N

Oh, isn't that cute?

T

Let's go to bed.

(*They tiptoe across the living room to the hallway, but about half way there, there is another electronic sound, a soft whirring and grinding noise.* NINA *stops and covers her ears.*)

N

(*a revelation*) Ah ha, the Van Horn's satellite dish. Zontal fixed it and now they're scanning with it.

T

(*pulling her back toward the patio*) Come on honey, let's go take care of that dish.

(*But before they can leave,* ZONTAL *awakes and paws at the swath of black mohair in which he's entangled.*)

Z

Ackk! What is this thing?

N

Oh my gosh, it's what was covering the Barca! Jackie, was it you?

J

No, I found it by the pool.

T

Bastards! They planted it on us. We're screwed.

Z

It's a piece of mohair fabric?

J

From the Crosby's Barcalounger. The Van Horns stripped it so that it would look like Tom and Nina were anti-social and get kicked off the program.

Z

(rises) Why didn't you just go and talk to them and say something like, 'Maybe you could tone it down, please?' It's the socializing goal of your program. *(Long beat while he produces a small notebook, flipping its pages.)* I'm going to give you a provisional advance recommendation.

TN

(long beat) Provisional advance recommendation! What the hell is that?

Z

You're eligible for the next phase of the program, but you don't get priority ranking.

T

Wait a minute – you're evaluating us?

Z

For NASA, right. I have a friend in command and since I know Nina, he asked me to look in on you all. Sorry I had to be so sneaky, but you'd didn't really think that they weren't going to check up on you, did you?

N
But we were friends?

Z
We still are, I hope.

T
That doesn't matter now. Just give us our scores.

Z
Well, you did very well on the family unit part of the test – conflict resolution, not so good – we give extra weight to social adaptability, because it's very important if you're locked up together in a community module parked near Alpha Centauri.

T
And, the Van Horns?

Z
They're probably out of the program.

T
All three of them?

Z
That's right, all three of them.

T
Conflict resolution?

N
If only we had known …

(TOM *puts his arm around* NINA'S *waist and pulls her closer. She snuggles up against him.*)

T

But that's just it, we didn't know ...

J

I think Zontal needs some fresh air, don't you all?

(JACKIE *grabs* ZONTAL'S *arm and leads him to the door.*)

Z

(waving) Goodbye.

(JACKIE *hesitates, but follows* ZONTAL. TOM *and* NINA *start toward the bedroom again, but* NINA *sits on the sofa, pulling* TOM *down with her, putting her feet in his lap for a foot rub. The noise of the satellite dish subsides and is replaced by softly chirping birds. The lights grow slowly brighter, then blackout.*)

Published on the occasion of William Leavitt's show *Sidereal Time* at gta exhibitions, ETH Zürich

Editors
Fredi Fischli, Niels Olsen

Author
William Leavitt

Photographs
William Leavitt

Editing
Andreas Koller

Proofreading
Claudio Cambon

Design
Teo Schifferli

Typeface
Programme

Edition Patrick Frey
Limmatstrasse 268
CH-8005 Zürich

www.editionpatrickfrey.com
mail@editionpatrickfrey.ch

All rights reserved. No part of this publication may be reproduced, stored on a retrieval system or transmitted in any form by any means whatsoever (including electronic, mechanical, microcopying, photocopying, recording or otherwise) without the prior permission in writing of the authors and the publisher.

First edition: STUDIOLO / Edition Patrick Frey, 2014
ISBN 978-3-905929-60-7

Distribution:
Edition Patrick Frey, www.editionpatrickfrey.com

© 2014 for texts and images: the author
© 2014 for this edition: Edition Patrick Frey

Printed in Lithuania